TRACK
ATTACK

GYM SHORTS

TRACK ATTACK

Betty Hicks

Illustrated by Simon Gane

ROARING BROOK PRESS
NEW YORK

Many thanks to expert runner William Hicks for reading my manuscript and sharing his track-and-field knowledge with me. —B.H.

Text copyright © 2009 by Betty Hicks
Illustrations copyright © 2009 by Simon Gane
Published by Roaring Brook Press
Roaring Brook Press is a division of
Holtzbrinck Publishing Holdings Limited Partnership
175 Fifth Avenue, New York, New York 10010
www.roaringbrookpress.com

Cataloging-in-Publication Data is on file at the Library of Congress
Hicks, Betty.
ISBN: 978-1-59643-488-2

Roaring Brook Press books are available for special promotions and premiums.
For details, contact: Director of Special Markets, Holtzbrinck Publishers.

Book design by Jennifer Browne
Printed in June 2009 in the United States of America
by Worzalla, Stevens Point, Wisconsin
First edition August 2009
2 4 6 8 10 9 7 5 3 1

For Austin

CONTENTS

SPIKES

Jazz sat in the sporting goods store beside her dad. Piles of track shoes lay heaped around her. All of them had spikes.

She felt as if she were surrounded by a bunch of those small man-eating fish that live in the Amazon River—the ones with the tiny, gnashing teeth.

"Dad," Jazz explained again, "these are so cool. But I don't need spikes. Coach wants us all to have plain running shoes. And my old ones are worn out."

"You're going to be *great* at track," said Dad. "Just wait till we get home. I'll show you how to—"

Jazz tuned him out. Ever since Jazz signed up for the track team, Dad had been excited about helping her. So excited he didn't listen.

Jazz looked to the salesclerk for help.

"We have some really nice running shoes," said the clerk.

"She doesn't need running shoes," said Dad. "She needs track shoes—with spikes."

The clerk shrugged his shoulders at Jazz.

"You can't get a fast start without spikes," Dad explained.

"Dad," Jazz exclaimed. "Coach said no spikes!"

"But . . . but," Dad sputtered. "Track shoes have had spikes for a hundred years. They were invented in 1920!"

Dad always knew stuff like that.

"Well," said Jazz, "in the 1960 Summer Olympics, a man won a gold medal *and* set a world record— running barefoot."

Jazz knew stuff, too.

"Really?" said Dad, his eyes opening wide. "No shoes?"

Finally! Dad heard something she'd said. "Right," Jazz nodded. "And for track, my age group wears running shoes. No spikes."

"Oh," said Dad. "Okay." He motioned to the clerk. "I guess we need to see your running shoes, please."

Jazz squeezed his hand. "Thanks, Dad."

"What if I talked to your coach about changing the spikes rule?"

"Dad!" exclaimed Jazz.

Everyone in the store stared.

"Do not go to my coach," Jazz whispered. "Not about rules. Not about spikes. Not about anything. Okay?"

Dad sighed. "Fine. But I do know about running. I can help you. I—"

Jazz pictured their den at home. A trophy case

covered one wall. It was filled with trophies of runners, pole-vaulters, and hurdlers. Her dad had won them all.

But Jazz didn't want a jillion trophies. She just wanted to sprint on a track team. Because when Jazz ran, she felt just like a lightning bolt.

Fast. Strong. Sizzling.

She was glad her dad cared about her sports. She just wished he didn't care quite so much.

CRAZY, LOONY, NUTS

Driving home from the shoe store, Jazz's dad smiled. He tapped his fingers in time with the music on the radio. "I can't wait to get home and help you practice your sprinting. I have this great idea about how to—"

"Dad, I'm not supposed to run today."

Dad frowned. "Not run? Are you kidding? You're on a *track* team—"

"I ran yesterday," said Jazz. "And I have practice again tomorrow. Coach wants us to rest our muscles today."

"Oh," said Dad as he pulled into their driveway. "Makes sense. But, what if we just did one little—"

"Dad," Jazz groaned.

"Okay! Okay!" Dad held up his hands as if he were being robbed. He parked the van and went inside.

Jazz slumped onto her back steps. Titan, her big, fluffy cat, circled figure eights around her leg. Had she hurt Dad's feelings? She hoped not.

Since her mom had died, Jazz's dad did everything. He cooked. He carpooled. He cleaned Titan's litter box, even though that was Jazz's job. He gave awesome birthday parties. He did her hair.

But sometimes he did too much.

"What's wrong?" asked Henry.

Jazz looked up.

Her friends Henry, Rocky, Rita, and Goose were there. All five of them lived in the same neighborhood. They had exactly enough people for a basketball team. Or any other sport they wanted to play.

"Dad's driving me crazy," said Jazz.

"*Crazy?*" echoed Henry.

"Yeah," said Jazz. She crossed her eyes and swirled her fingers around in front of her ears. "Crazy. Loony. Nuts."

"How about a Tootsie Pop?" asked Goose.

Goose thought Tootsie Pops could fix anything. He patted down all his pockets, trying to find one.

"I'm not hungry," Jazz answered.

"Hungry!" Goose waved his arms in alarm. "Tootsie Pops aren't about hunger. They're about taste! And sugar. And—"

Rocky elbowed Goose. "Chill *out*," he whispered.

"Oh. Yeah. Sorry, Jazz," said Goose. He stuffed his hands in his pockets. "So what's the deal with your dad?"

"Okay," said Jazz. "you know how excited he's been about me running track?"

They all nodded.

"Well, he won't stop talking about it long enough to listen. Today he wanted to buy me spikes. Then he wanted me to practice when I'm not supposed to." Jazz sighed. "He's having a track attack."

Rita, who loved to move like a ballet dancer, twirled on one toe and swung her arms in a circle. "So," she said, "did you tell him you don't need spikes?"

"Of *course* I told him," said Jazz. "I told him fifty times." She held up ten fingers and wiggled them around a lot, trying to make them look like more.

"You're so lucky," said Henry. "I would love to have spikes."

Henry was such a sports nut, he had almost every kind of shoe there was. He had soccer shoes, tennis shoes, cross trainers, his cousin's old ski boots, a pair of used golf shoes, and his very own ice skates. He even had a pair of way-too-big bowling shoes he found at a garage sale.

"I wish my dad got that pumped about sports," Henry added.

"I wish my dad didn't," said Jazz. "I mean, he even wanted to ask Coach to change the rules."

"What!" Jazz's friends let out a group gasp.

Having a parent who came to games and liked sports was a good thing. But asking a coach to change rules—for his own kid? *Whoa!* There was no word for how awful that was.

TWO-WAY SIZZLE

The next day, Dad dropped Jazz at practice. She ran as fast as she could toward the track. She loved her new running shoes. She had tested them at home that morning. She could go from standing still to *whoosh* in two seconds flat.

She didn't even care if she won. She just loved to run.

Jazz joined the crowd of kids waiting for practice to start.

"Cool shoes," said Rocky.

"Thanks," said Jazz. She held up one foot to show off her shoe. She couldn't wait to run some more. She looked around for Coach.

He was standing near the parking lot, talking to Dad!

Was Dad talking about spikes? He promised he wouldn't!

Jazz felt like a lightning bolt again. Not because she was sizzling fast. No. Because she was sizzling mad.

"I bet Coach makes us run till we barf," said Goose.

Jazz thought she might barf without the running.

Had Dad asked Coach to change the rules?

If he had, would Coach be mad at *her*?

Coach strolled over to the team. He flashed a big grin and said, "Okay! Everybody ready?"

Jazz relaxed. Coach didn't seem annoyed—he seemed happy. So, whatever Dad had said, she was *not* going to let it bother her, either.

"This is our last practice before our first meet," said Coach. "Today you'll need to decide what event you want to enter."

Jazz already knew. She wanted to run the 100 meters, because she got to sprint as fast as she could. Fifteen seconds and the race was over—no need to pace herself. Jazz hated pacing herself, because she had only one speed—zoom. The 100 was perfect.

"I want to do the shot put," whispered Rocky.

"Javelin throw," said Goose.

"I'm doing *everything*," said Henry. "Shot put, long jump, sprints, distance runs, cross country—"

"You can't do *all* that," said Rita.

Poor Henry, thought Jazz. How would he ever decide?

"Okay," said Coach, "let's warm up with a slow jog around the track."

Jazz took off like a jet.

"Slow down!" Coach called after her. "Warm up your muscles first."

Jazz slowed to a trot. She focused on the tempo of her arms and legs. She wished Coach would let her run faster.

Next, everyone stretched. Jazz placed one hand against a bench for balance. She used the other hand to lift her foot up against the back of her leg. She felt a stretch in the front of her thigh.

"I love quad stretches," she said, smiling.

Goose was doing the same thing. "Until I signed up for track," he moaned, "I didn't know I had a quad."

"I didn't know I had a hamstring," said Rita. She sat on the ground with her legs straight out in front of her. She leaned forward and stretched the muscle in the back of her leg.

Jazz switched legs, stretching her other thigh. As her muscles loosened up, she noticed how clear the sky was and how nice the sun felt. And how Dad seemed a long way away.

ALL TIED UP

While Jazz did her stretches, she watched Coach show other team members some new moves.

One girl skipped with her knees so high, Jazz thought she looked like a marching-band leader gone bonkers. A boy did something called the grapevine, crossing one foot over the other, moving sideways, and twisting.

"I want to try that!" exclaimed Rita. In seconds, she was stepping like a pro. Arms left, arms right, left foot behind the right. All her curly hair bouncing. All her moves smooth.

Henry and Rocky tried to copy Rita. But they tripped and fell in a tangled heap, laughing.

"Jazz!" said Coach. "Come here, please."

Jazz ran over. She couldn't wait to see what he would teach *her*.

Coach pulled a bungee cord out of his duffel bag. "I'm going to tie you up," he said.

Tie me up? thought Jazz.

Slowly, Coach wrapped the cord around Jazz, pinning down her arms.

Jazz tried not to laugh. But she couldn't help it. A coach tying up a kid? How silly was that?

"Now, run to the bench as fast as you can," said Coach.

Jazz ran. It felt strange. She couldn't get going. She didn't know whether to bend forward, stand straight, or fall down.

"Rita," called Coach. "Untie Jazz."

Rita unwound the cord and whispered, "This is so weird."

"*Now* run," said Coach.

Jazz took off as if she'd been popped out of a slingshot. "You need arms to run!" she exclaimed.

"Exactly," said Coach. "Anyone else want to try?"

More kids took turns. They ran. Some fell down. Some acted goofy. Goose and Rocky pretended they were mummies.

Then Coach said, "Okay. We just learned our arms help us run. Now, let's practice pumping them in time with our legs.

Jazz did it right on the first try. Her arms and legs had perfect timing. Coach said so.

He also told everyone not to worry if they weren't the fastest. "Work on being fast*er*," he said. "Beating your own best time is as good as a win."

"Coach is so cool," said Rocky.

"He's awesome," said Jazz.

TRACK ATTACK

Jazz arrived at her first meet excited about running. Her belly felt full of jumping beans.

Her stomach was actually full of spaghetti. Two hours earlier, Dad had cooked a big bowl of pasta for her.

"Carbs," he said, "are good to eat before a race."

After she ate, he asked her to stand up.

Jazz stood.

"Okay," said Dad. "Fall forward."

"You want me to fall?" asked Jazz.

Dad nodded.

Jazz shrugged and toppled forward. Her right leg swung out to stop her fall.

"Aha!" exclaimed Dad. "That's your quick leg. The right one. Place it behind the left one to start your race."

Sometimes Jazz was glad her dad knew things about running.

At the meet, the field was covered with kids—all of them doing different warm-ups. Energy crackled through Jazz like sparks.

She and her friends helped her dad unload the snacks he told Coach he'd bring. They carried oranges, cups, and a cooler to their team's meeting area.

Goose pawed through the cooler. He turned all the cups upside down. "What? No Tootsie Pops?"

Jazz's dad pulled one grape Tootsie Pop out of his pocket, just for Goose.

A loudspeaker blared out times and events. Coach trotted from one person to another, announcing last-minute changes. Goose, Jazz, Rocky, Henry, and Rita formed a huddle and wished each other luck.

Then they jogged slowly around the track to warm up.

"Hey!" Dad called after them. "You should stretch first."

Jazz pretended not to hear. Coach said it's better to stretch *after* you jog.

"Why am I running?" asked Goose.

"Duh," said Henry. "It's a track team."

Goose groaned. "I hate to run. All I want to do is throw a javelin."

"Running's good for your heart," said Rita.

"Heart's fine." Goose panted. "It's my breath I'm worried about."

Five minutes ago, Jazz would have laughed. Now, she was too busy wondering if she should explain to Dad what Coach had taught them about warm-ups.

Don't think about Dad, she decided.

She began her stretches for the 100-meter dash.

"Remember," said Dad, walking over to her, "you need a fast start."

Jazz nodded as she stretched her calf muscles. Why was he still on the field?

"Better practice a few minutes on the starting blocks," said Dad.

"I don't use a starting block," she muttered.

"What!" Dad exclaimed. "You *have* to." He whipped his head right and left, looking for one. "You can't

win sprints without a fast start. The other runners will—"

"Please, Dad," whispered Jazz. "*None* of the nine and tens use starting blocks. We do a standing start."

"Oh." Dad blinked. He fluttered his fingers.

"Dad," said Jazz. "You have to leave the field now. No parents allowed."

"Don't move before the starting gun," Dad added. Then he began to walk toward the bleachers. "Or you'll be DQed," he called back over his shoulder.

Jazz wanted to say, *I know that*, but she just nodded. Everybody knows you can't move after you're set or you'll be disqualified.

"Relax your fingers. Don't make a fist," he called from his seat on the front row.

"And *don't*—"

Jazz pretended not to hear. Dad might have been a

super track star, but he was a terrible coach. Too many *don'ts*. She chanted under her breath, "I can. I can. I can."

The loud speaker blared, "One hundred meters, nine and ten girls."

"Get out there and win!" said Dad, waving his arms.

Jazz and four other runners jogged over to the track. Jazz took her stance in lane three— strongest leg forward, quickest leg back. More weight on the front leg. Eyes focused ten meters down the track.

"Go Jazz!" yelled Dad.

She wished he wouldn't cheer yet. The other fans were still quiet. The race hadn't even started!

Jazz told the jumping beans in her belly to chill out. She wished the starter would hurry up.

Be still. Be ready.

Come on! Start!

"On your marks," said the starter.

I'm on my mark, thought Jazz.

"Set," said the starter.

I am set, thought Jazz. She was ready to explode. She bent an inch lower.

"Pop! Pop!" The gun fired twice to signal a false start. The starter pointed to Jazz.

Jazz felt as if she'd been hit by a fist. All the energy whooshed out of her body.

"What!" shouted Dad. "Are you blind? Are you nuts? She never moved!"

Dad leaped up from the bleachers and marched onto the track.

"Sir," said the ref. "You'll have to leave the track area."

Dad ignored the warning. "She never moved!"

"Dad," whispered Jazz, "I *did* move."

"You did? But . . . but . . . didn't I warn you not to? Didn't you hear me?"

Coach squeezed Jazz's shoulder. "It's okay," he said. Then he took Jazz's father by the arm and politely steered him off the field.

SECOND CHANCE

"On your marks," said the starter.

Jazz got ready.

"Set."

Jazz took her stance. She didn't move. She didn't even breathe.

She had been given another chance—sprinters are allowed one false start.

Her dad got one more chance, too. But the ref said that if he walked onto the field again, he'd have to leave the meet.

Jazz focused on her race. If she thought about what her dad had done, she would cry.

"Pop!" went the starter's gun.

Jazz took off. Instantly, she was upright. Arms pumping. Big, strong moves. Running as fast as she could.

Don't look back. Halfway there. Finish line. Closer. Closer. Closer.

Jazz pulled both arms back. Her head and shoulders dipped forward. Her chest broke the tape.

She had won!

Rocky, Rita, and Henry ran over. "Way to go!" they cheered.

Goose was on the other side of the field, competing in the javelin throw.

Jazz bent over, gasping for breath.

"You won!" shouted Rita.

"Did you see"—she gulped for air—"what Dad did?"

"Yeah, but it's okay," said Henry. "He just gets excited."

Rocky and Rita nodded.

Jazz knew they were trying to make her feel better. But it wasn't working.

Riding home in the van after the meet, Dad told Jazz and her friends, "I'm sorry I yelled at the referee. I got carried away."

Rocky, Rita, Henry, and Goose all muttered, "That's okay." "Don't worry." "No problem."

"It's *not* okay," said Dad. "I lost my cool."

Jazz squeezed her fists until they ached.

The van filled up with silence—the kind that's loud and makes everyone feel itchy all over.

"I'm sorry, Jazz," Dad repeated when they got home.

Jazz went straight to her room. She curled up on her bed with Titan. Huge tears floated in her eyes. They spilled over onto Titan's fur.

Quickly, Jazz swiped away the drops—Titan hated being wet.

Suddenly, Jazz had an idea. She bolted up so fast, Titan flipped off the bed.

"Sorry." Jazz stroked Titan. Then she sat on the floor and flipped through her books. She had books on everything. *Jousting. The Truth About Pirates. All You Ever Wanted to Know About Elephants.* Books that answered every question there was. Who invented movies? Why are polar bears white? Can birds have hiccups?

Jazz scanned the indexes of three stacks of books. Titan hid under her bed. But there wasn't a single book that said anything about how to control a too-excited dad.

"Jazz," called Dad. "I have a surprise for you!"

What now? thought Jazz.

She found Dad standing in front of their open freezer. He held up a quart of Butterfinger ice cream. Jazz's favorite.

She hugged him. What else could she do? He was a great dad.

Jazz just hoped he wouldn't come to her next meet.

TRACK TRICKS

Two days later, Dad dropped off Jazz at the track. He was too busy at work to watch any more practices for a while. "Sorry I can't stay," he said.

Jazz's eyes sparkled. "No problem."

Out on the field, Coach pulled the sprinters aside to show them a trick to prevent false starts. He said they were going to boost the timer in their brains.

"Rita," said Coach. "We know you can run fast. Let's see how fast you can think."

Coach dangled a ruler in the space just above Rita's thumb and pointer finger. "When I drop the ruler, catch it."

Rita shrugged. "Okay."

Coach let the ruler go. Rita pinched her fingers together—too late. The ruler dropped to the ground.

"Whoa!" said Rita. "Can I try again?"

This time, when Coach dropped it, she caught the tip just as it was about to slip through again.

"Now," said Coach. "*You* drop the ruler."

Rita held the ruler, let go, and caught it almost instantly. "Woo-hoo!" she cheered, and twirled on one toe.

"When *you* drop it," said Coach, "you react fast, because you know it's coming. When *I* drop it, your brain has to see it, *then* tell your muscles to grab."

Rita dropped the ruler for Jazz.

Jazz missed it.

"It's like waiting for the starter's gun. Someone else starts the action," explained Coach.

Jazz was having fun trying to catch the ruler. "Do-over," she begged Rita.

Coach had everyone practice quick starts until they all reacted faster—with no false starts.

Jazz loved it. She got to take off running. Over and over.

This was why she signed up for track.

PAIN

For two weeks, Jazz hung out with her friends. She went to practice. She felt like a lightning bolt.

But on the day of her next meet, she felt like a beehive. A million tiny wings flapped inside her stomach, churning her spaghetti lunch.

Dad had been talking nonstop for an hour—at home, in the van, and now, at the meet. "Don't be too tight. Don't be too loose. Don't let your feet flop. Always make contact with the ball of your foot. Don't—"

Jazz stepped up to the line for the 100. Dad stood right up against the fence that ran beside the bleachers—as close to her as he could get. Waving his arms. Cheering his head off. Screaming, "You can win!"

"On your marks."

Jazz got ready.

"Set."

Jazz got set.

"Pop!"

Jazz exploded forward. She ran. Fast. Focused. The tiny wings vanished. Jazz was nothing but pumping arms. Pounding feet. A bolt of lightning.

Do it. Do it. Faster. Faster.

The runner in the next lane is close. Too close! She's in my lane!

Jazz's foot struck something.

No!

Jazz felt herself falling. Her knee skidded across the track surface. Her palm slammed into dirt.

"She was tripped!" screamed Dad.

Jazz slumped on the track and watched blood trickle down her leg. Her knee hurt. Her hand hurt.

Coach rushed over. "Are you okay?"

Coach helped her up. "That runner—was she in your lane?"

"Yes. No. I don't know," said Jazz. She rubbed her palm where it throbbed. It happened so fast, she wasn't sure.

Dad ran toward her. "Are you hurt?"

"I'm fine." She stood and brushed dirt off her running shorts.

Dad turned to the ref. "That girl"—he pointed at the winning runner—"she tripped my daughter. She should be DQed."

"Sir, I'm sorry. But I didn't see any foul," said the ref.

"Well, maybe you need glasses," Dad muttered under his breath.

"Dad, please," said Jazz. "Let Coach handle it."

"You should run the race over," said Dad.

"*Sir,*" said the ref, "you need to return to the bleachers."

"Who else saw this race?" Dad called out, looking around for witnesses.

Everyone was staring at Jazz's dad.

"No one saw any contact," said Coach, putting his hand gently on Dad's shoulder. "Jazz isn't even sure—"

Dad raised his voice. "Didn't anybody see—?"

"I'm sorry, sir," said the ref, "but I'm going to have to ask you to leave the meet."

Jazz wanted to run straight down the track and never stop—all the way home and into her room.

That's Not Funny

Jazz sat on the field while a medic washed grit out of her scraped knee. Dad waited for her in the van.

Jazz gaped at the gauze bandage being applied to her leg. She tried not to cry—not because it hurt. No, because her dad had been asked to leave the meet.

When the medic finished, Rita and Henry sat on the grass beside Jazz. Rocky and Goose plopped down in front of her.

"You all know what happened to Dad?" asked Jazz, her voice cracking.

"He was just trying to help," said Rocky. "He thought you'd been fouled."

"Yeah," said Henry. "He thought it wasn't fair."

"That's *Coach's* job," said Jazz.

"But your dad's still great," said Rita, holding up a box of lemon drops. "Look what he gave me for winning the long jump." Rita loved lemon drops.

"And he made sugar cookies for us to eat after the meet," said Henry. "He told me."

"I wish *my* dad baked cookies," said Rocky. "Your dad is so cool."

"Except when he's hot," said Goose, grinning his goofball grin. He looked from one friend to another to make sure they got the joke.

"That's not funny, not even a little," said Rita.

"You're right," said Goose. "Sorry."

Jazz sighed. "No problem." She knew Goose hadn't meant to be mean. But still . . . there *was* a problem. Dad.

Jazz was great at solving other people's problems.

When Rocky broke his arm playing baseball, she helped him get over his fear. She helped Rita with swimming and Goose with soccer. Why couldn't she help herself?

"Track's no fun anymore," said Jazz. "I hate it."

"Your dad just gets excited," said Rocky.

"No kidding," groaned Jazz.

"Talk to him," said Rita.

"And say what?" asked Jazz. "That he embarrasses me? That Coach is a better coach than he is? That he cheers too loud? That—"

"Well, yeah," said Rita. "Only say it nicer so you don't hurt his feelings."

"He wouldn't listen," answered Jazz. "He'd be too pumped up, telling me about the history of spikes, or the value of starting blocks, or—"

"You have to find the right time," said Rocky.

"He's right." Rita nodded. "Don't talk to him when he's late for work."

"Or when he's just seen your report card," said Henry.

"Or when you just squished a bunch of blueberries

into the sofa cushion," said Goose.

Jazz had to laugh. But hey! Maybe they were right.

Only, what would she say? Deep down, Jazz knew
there was only one thing she *could* say—*Dad, do not
come to my meets anymore.*

SPIT IT OUT

Jazz had stared at her bandaged knee and wondered when she would *ever* find the right time to talk to Dad.

Riding home from the meet had not been a good time. Her friends were in the car.

Talking to him after they got home had not been a good time. He had to cook dinner.

And now, talking to him *at* dinner wasn't a good time, either. After all, it was bad manners to talk with her mouth full. Okay—that was a lame reason. Who was Jazz kidding? She just didn't *want* to tell him.

She sat at dinner and scraped all the mushrooms off her chicken. Even if she liked mushrooms, she wouldn't have eaten them.

She couldn't even look at him. With her head down, she took a deep breath. "Uh . . . Dad . . ." *Spit it out.*

Get it over with. Just tell him. "Dad . . . um . . . I don't
. . . um . . . want you to come to my meets anymore."

The silence wasn't itchy. It was heavy. Jazz felt it
pressing on her head, her shoulders, her everything.
Like cement. Or an elephant. Maybe even a planet.

"But, Jazz," Dad said finally. His voice sounded
sad. "I was trying to help you."

"But you argued with the ref. And you stayed on the field." Jazz put down her fork and looked directly into his eyes. "You're not the coach."

"Jazz!" exclaimed Dad. "That girl was in your lane! She made you fall. You would have *won*."

"Dad. Listen. I don't *care* if I win."

"You don't care if you win!"

"Well . . ." Jazz shrugged. "Winning's great. But that's not why I run. Besides, Coach says beating your best time is as good as a win."

Dad looked at her. His eyeballs moved from side to side in quick jerks, as if he were working hard math problems in his head. "I have to think about this," he said. He stared at Jazz's plate.

She was afraid he was going to tell her to eat her mushrooms. But he didn't. Instead, he said, "Getting asked to leave the meet made you ashamed of me. I won't set foot on the field again. I promise."

Jazz slumped. He still didn't get it.

She saw the pain in his face though, and she knew he would try to stay off the field. But could he? And what about all the track advice he gave her that was *not* helpful, and the too-loud cheering? She couldn't ask him to change those things, too. Hadn't she already hurt his feelings enough? Jazz wished she'd never joined the track team.

"Look," said Dad, "if you see me even *thinking* about walking onto the field or arguing with the ref, you can glue my legs together. You can cut out my tongue—"

"Dad," said Jazz, "that's gross."

"Come on." He squeezed her arm gently. "One more chance?"

Jazz stabbed a mushroom. What choice did she have? "Okay," she said. "One more chance."

LAST CHANCE

At the next meet, Dad wore a T-shirt that said "I ♥ Jazz." He hugged her and said, "Don't DQ."

Jazz nodded. She watched him walk away toward the bleachers. She nibbled on her fingernail and hoped he would stay there.

Coach gave her a pat on the back and said, "Run your best."

Jazz wished Dad was more like Coach. *And* she wished Dad didn't have her name on his shirt.

Coach waved to her dad. "Your dad's great," said Coach. "Really helpful. Did you know that the run-with-no-arms trick was his idea?"

No, Jazz did not know.

"And he told me how sorry he was for making a scene at the last meet."

He did? thought Jazz as she stepped into lane 2 for the 100.

"Go, Jazz!" screamed Dad.

Jazz forced a fake smile, then put her head down. *Coach thinks Dad is great. My friends think Dad is great.*

"On your marks."

Jazz got ready. *Don't think about Dad.*

"Set."

Jazz got set.

"Pop! Pop!"

False start! The starter pointed toward Jazz.

What! I didn't move. I know I didn't. Oh, no! Jazz was afraid to look at Dad.

Slowly, she turned her head. Dad waved from the bleachers. "I'm okay," he signaled. He pointed to his lap. He had strapped himself into his seat with a bungee cord.

He tied himself to his seat? It wasn't exactly what Jazz had hoped for. She stared. He must have done it as a joke. Right?

Dad grinned and winked.

Jazz stifled a giggle.

Then she felt excited. Dad finally got it. Well . . . at least *some* of it.

"Go, Jazz!" he yelled.

All of a sudden, Jazz got it, too—what her friends had been saying for weeks. What Coach had just said. Maybe Dad *was* great.

Okay—he cheered too loud. And he coached all wrong. But he did a lot of things right.

"On your marks."

Jazz cleared her head. She toed the starting line. Her last chance. *Do not DQ.*

She held her left arm forward, her right arm back. Relaxed hands. No fists.

"Get set."

Jazz got set. She didn't move. Not even a hair.

"*Pop!*"

Jazz bolted forward into the lane. Upright. A good start. No. A great start! She pumped her arms and legs and ran as fast as she'd ever run in her life.

She heard her friends and her dad screaming, "Go, Jazz. Go!"

Her heart tingled. Her arms pumped. Her feet flew.

The finish line. Closer. Closer. Almost there.

Jazz grinned. She felt exactly like a lightning bolt.

Fast. Strong. Sizzling.

Exactly the way she was supposed to feel.

FIC
HIC

Hicks, Betty.

Track attack.

Gr 2-4

$15.99

39545000736081